Henry and Mudge
AND THE
Forever Sea

The Sixth Book of Their Adventures

Story by Cynthia Rylant

Pictures by Suçie Stevenson

Aladdin Paperbacks

To Cheryl and Marc — CR
For Walker — SS

Aladdin Paperbacks
An imprint of Simon & Schuster
Children's Publishing Division
1230 Avenue of the Americas
New York, NY 10020
Text copyright © 1989 by Cynthia Rylant
Illustrations copyright © 1989 by Suçie Stevenson

First Aladdin Paperbacks edition, 1993
Also available in a hardcover edition from Macmillan Books for Young Readers

Printed in the United States of America
10 9 8 7 6 5 4

The text of this book is set in 18 pt. Goudy Old Style.

The illustrations are rendered in pen-and-ink and watercolor, reproduced in full color.

Library of Congress Cataloging-in-Publication Data

Rylant, Cynthia.
    Henry and Mudge and the forever sea : the sixth book of their adventures
    story by Cynthia Rylant : pictures by Suçie Stevenson.
    —1st Aladdin Books ed.
        p.   cm.
    Summary: Follows the seaside adventures of Henry, Henry's father, and
Henry's big dog Mudge.
    ISBN 0-689-71701-6
    [1. Seashore—Fiction. 2. Dogs—Fiction. 3. Fathers and sons—
Fiction.] I. Stevenson, Suçie, ill. II. Title.
[PZ7.R982Hf 1993]
[E]—dc20   92-28646

Contents

To the Beach

It was summer vacation
and Henry and his big dog Mudge
were going to the beach.
Mudge had never been
to the beach.

Henry promised
he would like it.
"You'll like the waves,"
he said.
"And the sand castles.
And the shells.
But don't drink the water!"
he warned.
"Too salty!"

They went in the car
with Henry's father.
In Henry's bag were
green goggles,
a yellow bucket,
an orange shovel,
and a dump truck.

In Mudge's bag were
a blue bowl,
a jug of water,
half of a bone,
and a tennis ball.

In Henry's father's bag were
a book about shells,
six towels,
and a red rubber lobster
he liked
to bring along.

They sang sea songs
all the way.
Henry's father said
"Yo-ho-ho"
about a hundred times.
Henry acted like a shark.
Mudge just wagged.
They couldn't wait
to get there.

The Forever Sea

"I see it!" Henry shouted.
The ocean was waiting.
It was blue
and white
and forever.

Henry's father
honked the car horn.
Mudge barked.
They parked the car
and ran for the sand.

Mudge got there first.
He ran right into
the water.
SPLASH!

Henry was second.

SPLASH!

Henry's father was third.

SPLASH!

The white foam
rushed
around their legs.
They laughed and hopped
and ran.

A big wave
knocked Henry down.
He rolled
all the way
back to shore.

"Wow," said Henry.
He got up
and ran back in.

Henry's father rode a wave like he was a surfboard.

He rode it
all the way
back to shore.
"Wow," he said.
He got up
and ran back in.

Mudge was not as brave
as Henry and Henry's father.
He just ran
along the edge.
He stayed out
of the big waves.

But still he got
so wet
that he looked like
a whale with legs.

They all played
a long time.

For lunch,
Henry and Mudge
and Henry's father
walked to a hot dog stand.

Henry had a hot dog
with ketchup.
Henry's father had a hot dog
with ketchup
and mustard
and onions
and slaw
and chili
and cheese.

"Yuck," said Henry.

Mudge had three hot dogs.

Plain.

In one gulp.

After lunch,
Henry and his father
began to build
a sand castle.

Henry made the moats.

Henry's father made the towers.

Mudge made a nice bed
and went to sleep.

When the castle was finished,
Henry's father
stuck his red rubber lobster
on the tallest tower.
Then he and Henry
clapped their hands.

Suddenly

a giant wave

washed far on the sand

and it covered everything.

It covered the moats.

It covered the towers.

It covered Mudge, who woke up.

"Oops," said Henry.

"Save that lobster!"
cried Henry's father.
The water was pulling it
out to sea.

Mudge ran and jumped
into the waves.
He caught the lobster
before it was lost forever.

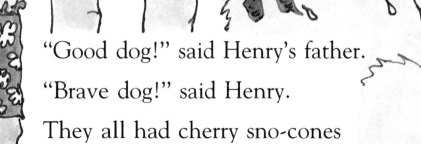

"Good dog!" said Henry's father.

"Brave dog!" said Henry.

They all had cherry sno-cones

to celebrate.

Good-bye, Crab

At the end of the day
it was time
to say good-bye
to the ocean.

Henry and Mudge
and Henry's father
walked along the sand,
watching the
orange sun set,
watching the
water sparkle
green and yellow.

Suddenly,
a crab popped out
from under the sand.
It came up sideways,
very fast.
So fast that Mudge
nearly stepped on it.

"Look out, Mudge!"
Henry said.
Mudge stopped
and put his nose
to the sand.
The crab looked at him.
He looked at the crab.

"I can't tell if that is
the front of the crab
or the back of the crab,"
said Henry's father.

Suddenly the crab ran,
sideways,
away from them.

Mudge chased it.
It popped back
under the sand.

Henry looked at its
new hole.
"Wow," he said.
"Wow," said his father.

Mudge stuck his nose
into the hole.
But nobody came out.

"Since we can't have
crab for dinner,"
said Henry's father,
"I guess we'll have
to have
another cherry sno-cone."

Henry cheered and hugged him.
As they walked down the sand,
Mudge stuck his nose
into every hole he saw.

But nobody

ever came out.